DISCARDED

Clarion Books
a Houghton Mifflin Company imprint
215 Park Avenue South, New York, NY 10003
Text and illustrations copyright © 2006 by Clavis Uitgeverij Amsterdam-Hasselt.
English language translation copyright © 2008 by Houghton Mifflin Company.

First published as *Benno Buitenspel* in Belgium in 2006 by Clavis Uitgeverij.
First American edition, 2008.

The illustrations were executed in oils.
The text was set in 22-point LT Tapeside.

www.clarionbooks.com

Printed in Italy.

Library of Congress Cataloging-in-Publication Data

Robberecht, Thierry.
[Benno buitenspel. English]
Sam is not a loser / by Thierry Robberecht ; illustrated by Philippe Goossens. — 1st American ed.
p. cm.
Summary: Sam loves to play games—even if he does not win every time.
ISBN 978-0-618-99210-2
[1. Winning and losing—Fiction. 2. Games—Fiction.] I. Goossens, Philippe, ill. II. Title.
PZ7.R53233Samg 2008
[E]—dc22
2007022116

10 9 8 7 6 5 4 3 2 1

Sam Is NOT a Loser

by Thierry Robberecht

Illustrated by Philippe Goossens

Clarion Books
New York

I'm Sam.

I love to play games.

But I don't like to lose—like I did tonight.

We played a card game, and my brother won.

I think my parents let him win because he's younger.

Last week, my friend Ray slept over.

We played Ping-Pong before dinner.

Ray didn't do very well.

But I did.

I won six games in a row!

After dinner, Mom played a game with us.

Mom and Ray got lucky the whole time.

But nothing went right for me.

It was so unfair!

Ray won the game.

"Great playing, Ray," Mom said.

Mom and Ray wanted to play again.

But I won't play if I'm not going to win.

I was so angry I knocked over the game

and ran to my room.

13

Mom came in to talk to me.

"You played well, too, Sam," she said.

"But you can't win every time."

I didn't speak to Ray for the rest of the night.

15

Saturday is soccer day.

But today we're playing against the big kids.

We'll never beat them.

I call Ray and tell him I won't be at the game.

"We need you!" Ray says.

"I have other things to do," I lie.

I want to play. But I don't want to lose.

17

Instead, I go to Grandma's house.

She always makes me feel better.

Today I tell her all about my soccer team while we play dominoes.

I win every game!

"Why aren't you at soccer today?" Grandma asks.

"I don't want to lose to the big kids," I tell her.

"But how can you win if you don't even play?" she says.

I never thought of that.

"I didn't win at dominoes," Grandma says.

"But I had fun seeing you and hearing about your team."

She takes out her photo album.

There are pictures of Mom and Dad, and my little brother.

And there's me, playing soccer!

"You always look so happy on the soccer field," Grandma says.

She's right. I do look happy.

And my team needs me.

23

"Can we get there in time for the game?" I ask.

Grandma smiles, and we rush to her car.

She drives like we're in a race.

And if we were, we'd have won!

"You made it!" Ray says when we get there.
"It wouldn't be Saturday without soccer,"
I tell him.
And we don't even lose the game—it ends
in a tie!
But the best part is that Ray is sleeping over
at my house again tonight.
This time we'll play a game we're both good at.

27

I'm Sam.

I love to play games—even if I don't win
every time.

But I still like to play dominoes with Grandma,
because I always win!